I0643758

The Book Thief

Lightbox Literature Studies

Tammy Gagne and Katie Gillespie

LIGHTBOX
openlightbox.com

LIGHTBOX

Go to
www.openlightbox.com
and enter this book's
unique code.

ACCESS CODE

LBXP7399

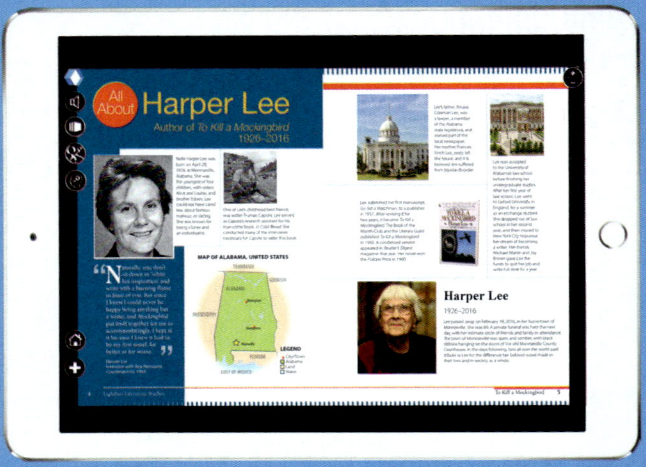

Lightbox is an all-inclusive digital solution for the teaching and learning of curriculum topics in an original, groundbreaking way. Lightbox is based on National Curriculum Standards.

STANDARD FEATURES OF LIGHTBOX

AUDIO High-quality narration using text-to-speech system

VIDEOS Embedded high-definition video clips

ACTIVITIES Printable PDFs that can be emailed and graded

WEBLINKS Curated links to external, child-safe resources

SLIDESHOWS Pictorial overviews of key concepts

TRANSPARENCIES Step-by-step layering of maps, diagrams, charts, and timelines

INTERACTIVE MAPS Interactive maps and aerial satellite imagery

QUIZZES Ten multiple choice questions that are automatically graded and emailed for teacher assessment

KEY WORDS Matching key concepts to their definitions

MORE Extra information and details on the subject

FIRST HAND Letters, diaries, and other primary sources

DOCS Speeches, newspaper articles, and other historical documents

Copyright © 2019 Smartbook Media Inc. All rights reserved.

Contents

NOW A MAJOR FILM FROM
TWENTIETH CENTURY FOX
'A novel of breath-taking scope, masterfully told' Guardian
MARKUS ZUSAK
The Book Thief
THE NUMBER ONE INTERNATIONAL BESTSELLER

RUBRIC

Conducting an Interview

Students will conduct an interview with a community member about a time period in their community's history, and submit an audio recording and transcript of the interview. An exemplary interview will meet the following criteria.

- Clearly defines the purpose of the interview
- Conducts thorough background research to inform the focus of the interview and the questions
- Drafts a complete list of thoughtful, in-depth, and varied questions prior to the interview
- Interviews a subject with relevant knowledge on the topic and time period in question
- Asks questions in a logical order, building upon each other
- Treats the interview subject in a polite, respectful, and professional manner
- Does not interrupt or rush the interview subject
- Shows interest and enthusiasm in responses and follow-up questions
- Chooses follow-up questions that demonstrate active listening
- Asks for clarification and further details when necessary
- Asks questions about personal experiences related to the topic
- Asks questions regarding factual information and the interview subject's opinion on the topic
- Asks creative questions that reflect fresh insights on the topic
- Records the full interview in a quiet environment
- Organizes and edits the interview transcript to be clear and factual

All About Markus Zusak

Author of *The Book Thief*

1975–

Markus Zusak grew up in Sydney, Australia, where he was born on June 23, 1975. His parents had immigrated to the island nation from Germany, in order to give their children a better life than they had had growing up. Zusak's command of the English language was apparent at a young age. He often wrote fiction for fun as a teenager, completing an as-yet unpublished novel at the age of 18. Although he worked as a high school English teacher for a while, he ultimately decided to turn his novel writing into a way to make a living.

> **"Once, when my computer was broken, I was writing the book I was working on at the time on foolscap paper. In the middle of it, I wrote a page about a girl stealing a book in modern-day Sydney. I didn't do anything with it at the time, but a few years later, when I started thinking seriously of writing about my parents and their childhoods in Germany and Austria during World War II, I thought, 'Maybe I should put that book thief in.' I guess that's how things start. You put two unrelated things together and at some point, you understand: they're actually not unrelated at all, they're perfect for each other."**
>
> Markus Zusak, *Interview with Heidi Stillman*, 2012

MAP OF GERMANY AND AUSTRALIA

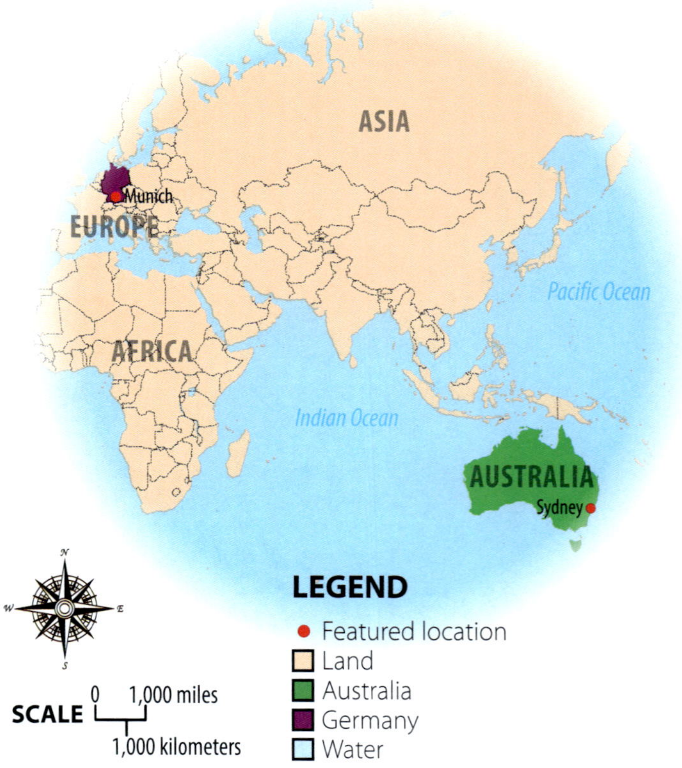

Since his first novel, *The Underdog*, was published in 1999, Zusak has been anything but an underdog in the field of publishing. This initial novel, as well as the two that soon followed, were well received in many places around the world. *Fighting Ruben Wolfe* and *Getting the Girl* rounded out the *Underdog* trilogy.

In addition to his native Australia, Zusak received praise and awards in Europe and the United States. His success was not the overnight variety, as he faced his share of rejection at first. However, once his books made it into the hands of readers, it was clear that they were interested in what the young Australian author had to say to them.

Zusak's fourth novel, *The Messenger*, was retitled *I Am the Messenger* in the United States. It also performed well with both readers and critics. He credits his ability to create engaging fiction for young adults to finding the right books to read himself as a young person. Zusak describes a good book as one that leaves him unaware that he is even turning its pages. When he is working on a novel, Zusak is often also in the midst of reading multiple books. He sees reading and writing as deeply connected activities.

The Book Thief, Zusak's fifth novel, was a significant departure from his previous works in more ways than one. First, it features a female main character, a young girl named Liesel Meminger. It also has a rather unique narrator, as the story itself is relayed by Death. Zusak based many of the events in the book on stories his parents had told about their time as children in Nazi Germany. First published in Australia in 2005, then released in the United States in 2006, *The Book Thief* has become Zusak's best-known novel to date.

ACTIVITIES

Google Maps

Munich, Germany

Explore the real-life city nearest the fictional setting of *The Book Thief*, using street view.

First Hand

Interview: Markus Zusak, author of The Book Thief

Examine this interview with Markus Zusak from June 5, 2014.

1. What types of questions does the interviewer ask? What topics does she focus on? Why would she focus on these specific areas?
2. Zusak says that he thinks "stories and words make us who we are," explaining that "[t]hey are what we carry around with us." How is this belief evidenced in *The Book Thief*? Give specific examples from the text.

RUBRIC

Researching for a Writing Assignment

Students will complete a thorough research process to prepare for a writing assignment, and organize their research in a logical manner that supports their writing. An exemplary research process will meet the following criteria.

- Creates a goal for the research, based on the topic and working thesis
- Creates specific, thoughtful, and inventive research questions that are relevant to the topic of the writing assignment
- Produces a list of categories, key words, and related ideas to effectively assist in researching
- Uses high-quality sources that pertain to the topic and come in a variety of formats, such as books, journals, primary sources, websites, and databases
- Determines accuracy of all sources
- Uses sources that provide balanced research and various perspectives on the topic in question
- Takes notes to highlight the key facts and ideas in order to answer all research questions
- Extracts relevant, detailed information from the sources during the note-taking process
- Organizes the research notes in a clear and concise manner
- Organizes the research notes logically and in a way that sets up the information and ideas for analysis and the writing process
- Analyzes the information and produces ideas and points to support the working thesis
- Uses an effective and suitable format to present all research
- Properly cites all sources used

Setting of the Novel

The Book Thief takes place in the fictional town of Molching, a suburb of Munich. After her younger brother Werner dies, Liesel is sent to live with a German sign painter and his wife, who become her new family. Hans and Rosa Hubermann reside at 33 Himmel Street, where much of the novel takes place. Liesel cannot read when she arrives in Molching. At school, this shortcoming forces her to be placed in a class with younger children, making her feel even more powerless over her life.

Snapshot

When Hitler **invaded Poland** in 1939, Britain and France declared war on Germany. This conflict, which also involved many other countries, ultimately escalated into **World War II**.

One of Hitler's **biggest goals** was creating what he saw as a superior race. His regime imprisoned or killed **millions of people** who did not fit this ideal.

Hitler blamed the **Jews** for Germany losing World War I. Through a horrific event known as the **Holocaust**, he ordered the murders of **more than 6 million Jews**.

The Basement

"For Max Vandenburg, there was cool cement and plenty of time to spend with it.
The minutes were cruel.
Hours were punishing.
Standing above him at all moments of awakeness was the hand of time, and it didn't hesitate to wring him out. It smiled and squeezed and let him live. What great malice there could be in allowing something to live.
At least once a day, Hans Hubermann would descend the basement steps and share a conversation. Rosa would occasionally bring a spare crust of bread. It was when Liesel came down, however, that Max found himself most interested in life again."

The Gamblers (A Seven-Sided Die)

Although Liesel is hesitant to trust the new people in her life at first, she grows closer to Hans, now Papa. He teaches her to read and write in the basement of their modest home when she cannot sleep. Since it is more private and somewhat hidden from the rest of the household, the cold, dark basement is also where the Hubermanns hide a young Jewish man from the Nazis. Images of Adolf Hitler and his Nazi agenda are everywhere, from the Nazi flags that residents are pressured to display to the **swastikas** on the uniforms of the school children. Many adults understand the ominous meaning of these images, but the children do not. They even sing Hitler youth songs at school without realizing how horrific the **anti-Semitic** lyrics are.

Much of the Nazi agenda was to control people's thoughts and opinions, particularly those about Hitler, the war, and the Jews. One way Hitler and his soldiers tried to accomplish this insidious task was through **censorship**. Words and ideas can be powerful, and the Nazis feared they would spread rapidly from one person to the next, making it harder for them to retain control of German citizens. The only things the Nazis wanted the people to read or see were materials that supported their agenda. Anything that could make the people question the party's ideology was deemed unacceptable.

ACTIVITIES

Video

The Book Thief: Emily Watson "Rosa" On Set Movie Interview

Examine this video interview with Emily Watson, who plays Rosa Hubermann in the film adaptation of the novel.

1. In the video, Watson refers to the setting of the story as "a very poor part of an ordinary town in Germany." Why is it significant that the Hubermanns live in this area? How might the plot change if the story were set in a richer neighborhood?
2. Why did Zusak choose to invent the fictional town of Molching as the setting for this story? What would be different if it were set in a real city? Could the story take place in any other country, besides Germany? Explain why you think so.

Weblink

Importance of Setting in a Novel

Review the article Nina Munteanu about the importance of setting in literature.

1. In the article, Munteanu says that setting includes three elements. What are these elements, and how does Zusak use them in *The Book Thief*? Explain how they come together to form the setting of the novel.
2. Munteanu talks about the link between setting and emotion. How does the setting of Zusak's novel amplify the emotions of the characters? Give specific examples from the novel.

RUBRIC

Analyzing a Video

Students will watch and assess a video related to a component of the novel, and write an analysis of the video. An exemplary video analysis will meet the following criteria.

- Identifies the purpose of the video
- Identifies the intended audience of the video
- Describes how the content of the video is presented
- Summarizes the information and opinions presented in the video
- Analyzes the quality of the content presented in the video
- Assesses the effectiveness of the video
- Discusses the technical aspects of the video and whether or not these enhance the content
- Determines whether the images and graphics used in the video relate to the content
- Determines whether the video is easy to follow and understand
- Gives the analysis a clear and consistent purpose
- Organizes the analysis in a logical, effective manner
- Presents a strong, clear argument about the video
- Provides strong and accurate details to support the argument about the video
- Considers other perspectives on the purpose and effectiveness of the video
- Makes connections between the video and the novel
- Properly integrates quotations from the video
- Cites all sources used in the analysis

Time Period of the Novel

The Book Thief takes place between 1939 and 1943, during World War II. The war cost more than 50 million people their lives, making it the deadliest war in history. More than 30 countries became involved in the conflict, which raged on until the Allies ultimately defeated Nazi Germany and Japan in 1945.

Hitler referred to himself as *Führer*, a title which means "leader" in German. Whether out of fear or devotion, the German people followed suit. Hitler's thirst for power and his malicious agenda had led to the rearmament of Germany despite the **Treaty of Versailles**. Britain, France, the United States, and Italy had forced Germany to sign this agreement at the end of World War I, but Hitler saw it as an attempt to destroy his country. He and his supporters decided early on that they would do whatever they could to undermine the treaty.

Terror in Molching

"As the years passed by, the Jews were being terrorized at random throughout the country, and in the spring of 1937, almost to his shame, Hans Hubermann finally submitted. He made some inquiries and applied to join the Party.

After lodging his form at the Nazi headquarters on Munich Street, he witnessed four men throw several bricks into a clothing store named Kleinmann's. It was one of the few Jewish shops that were still in operation in Molching."

The Accordionist (The Secret Life of Hans Hubermann)

The Treaty of Versailles inspired many Germans to adopt a fierce nationalism that helped Hitler become one of the most powerful dictators of the twentieth century. He convinced his followers that the Jews and other groups posed a threat to his supreme Aryan race. He soon began forcing these innocent people into **concentration camps**, where they were starved, tortured, and killed. Not all Germans supported the dictator, but most were too afraid to outwardly oppose him. Nonetheless, some Germans helped Jewish people by hiding them in their homes.

Growing up in Austria and Germany, Zusak's parents were about the same age as Liesel at the time of World War II. It was their stories about the time period which inspired Zusak to set the novel in World War II Germany, a choice that triggered many of the novel's themes. He has said that hearing their tales was like a piece of Europe had entered the family's kitchen. As awful as some of the stories were, they also relayed the happy memories from their childhoods. The Zusaks told their children about bombings and horrible sadness, but also friendships and laughter, as all of these things created the backdrop for their adolescence.

The Zusaks had remarkably different childhoods than the ones their children enjoyed in Australia. As they shared their stories, the Zusaks recalled how children would offer bread to starving prisoners who were being forced to move to concentration camps. They also remembered how parents were punished if they did not allow their children to be taken to special schools run by the Nazi Party. As Zusak got older, he realized that he should share these stories with the rest of the world through his writing.

ACTIVITIES

Video

Interview with Markus Zusak, author of The Book Thief

Discover some of the real-life events that inspired Zusak's novel by watching this video.

1. In the video, Zusak recounts memories of his parents' stories about their lives in Munich and Austria during World War II. How might the childhood memories he describes have impacted his portrayal of the events in the novel? Give specific examples from the text.
2. How did the time period that *The Book Thief* was written in impact Zusak's creation of the novel? In what ways might the story be different if it were written during the war?

Document

THE BOOK THIEF BY Marcus Zusak HISTORICAL EVENTS – CHRONOLOGICAL TIMELINE

Examine the timeline to learn more about the historical events referred to in the novel.

1. Although *The Book Thief* is fictional, it is based on real places and events. Nazi book burnings, such as the one Liesel attends, actually occurred in Berlin, Germany, in 1933. What does Liesel's theft of a book from the ceremony reveal about her character? How does this act impact the way readers view Liesel?
2. Why do you think Zusak chose to feature Olympic gold medalist Jesse Owens in the story? What does Rudy's admiration of Owens reveal about him as a character?

Conflict in the Novel

Conflict is what drives a story forward and keeps the reader eager to find out how it ends. Early in a novel, the main character, or protagonist, typically encounters a major impediment of some sort. Sometimes, this problem comes from another person called the antagonist, but conflict can also arise from other sources, such as society as a whole, nature, or even the story's protagonist.

The Four Major Types of Conflict in Literature

In *The Sisterhood of the Traveling Pants*, by Ann Brashares, two of the teenage protagonists face man-versus-man conflicts. Carmen is in conflict with her divorced father, who has decided to remarry. On a summer trip to Greece, Lena finds herself having to choose between standing up to her strong-minded grandparents or losing her beloved, Kostas.

In John Green's *The Fault in Our Stars*, the main character is a teenage girl named Hazel who is fighting cancer. As she deals with the day-to-day struggles of her illness, and falls in love with another young cancer patient named Augustus, Hazel must face the possibility that she may not live the long life she once thought she would.

In *To Kill a Mockingbird*, by Harper Lee, the protagonist is a girl named Scout, who lives in Maycomb, Alabama, in the early 1930s. Her father, Atticus Finch, is a lawyer who agrees to defend an African American man named Tom Robinson, which outrages many members of the small town. **Society** poses the biggest conflict, with its collective **discrimination** against Robinson and African Americans in general.

In *Island of the Blue Dolphins*, by Scott O'Dell, the book's protagonist, a young girl named Karana, is left on an island with her brother, Ramo. The siblings successfully work together for a while, but when Karana discovers that a pack of wild dogs have killed Ramo, she is left to care for and feed herself. She must find a way to survive alone until she is able to get off the island.

RUBRIC

Writing a Short Story

Students will choose an excerpt from the novel and use it as their inspiration in writing a short story. An exemplary short story will meet the following criteria.

- Engages the reader from the opening line
- Establishes a clear, consistent point of view
- Introduces a narrator and a setting
- Develops an engaging conflict at the heart of the narrative to build tension and keep the reader interested
- Develops characters and events through purposeful and well-crafted literary devices
- Creates a logical progression of events in the narrative that build upon each other using various techniques
- Explores ideas, concepts, and writing styles with creativity and originality
- Demonstrates a high level of skill in using appropriate narrative techniques to tell the story
- Concludes the narrative in a thoughtful, effective manner appropriate to the narrative
- Uses varied, purposeful diction and syntax to affect style and serve the narrative
- Writes with clarity, imagination, and a unique, personal voice
- Does not use stereotypes or clichés
- Uses effective, believable dialogue
- Uses correct spelling, grammar, and punctuation

Types of Conflict in *The Book Thief*

The two main types of conflict in *The Book Thief* are man versus self and man versus society. Each of these conflicts propels the story forward.

Man versus Self

"It was June. It was Germany.

Things were on the verge of decay.

Liesel was unaware of this. For her, the Jew in her basement had not been revealed. Her foster parents were not taken away, and she herself had contributed greatly to both of these accomplishments.

'Everything's good,' she said, and she was not talking about a soccer injury of any description.

She was fine."

The Schmunzeler

Liesel

Man versus Society

"According to Papa, Rosa melted next to the stove the moment the party man was gone. They collected Liesel and made their way to the basement, removing the well-placed drop sheets and paint cans. Max Vandenburg sat beneath the steps, holding his rusty scissors like a knife. His armpits were soggy and the words fell like injuries from his mouth.
'I wouldn't have used them,' he quietly said.
'I'm...' he held the rusty arms flat against his forehead. 'I'm so sorry I put you through that.'
Papa lit a cigarette. Rosa took the scissors.
'You're alive,' she said. 'We all are.'
It was too late for apologies."

The Visitor

Rosa

Max

ACTIVITIES

More

The Types of Conflict in *The Book Thief*

Analyze the excerpts from the novel revealing the types of conflict as they appear in *The Book Thief*.

1. How do these excerpts of conflict reveal the novel's theme? How do they reveal character? Explain and defend your ideas.
2. Write an analysis of Zusak's development of Liesel's internal conflict. What deeper truths may be suggested about this character as a result of this conflict?

Video

Conflict in Literature

Explore the four different kinds of literary conflicts in this video.

1. Explain each of the four types of conflicts in your own words. Provide examples of each. They can be from plays, novels, short stories, films, or television shows.
2. What is the difference between an internal conflict and an external conflict? Can you think of any similarities between them?

RUBRIC

Holding a Classroom Debate

Students will form groups and prepare arguments for a debate on a controversial issue. Exemplary performance in a debate will meet the following criteria.

- Demonstrates in-depth understanding of the topic and related information
- Presents strong, logical, and convincing arguments
- Communicates in a clear and confident manner
- Maintains eye contact
- Uses clear vocal tone and a reasonable rate of vocal delivery
- Uses respectful and appropriate language and body language
- Delivers arguments, evidence, and counter-evidence in an engaging and persuasive manner
- Supports each major point of an argument with several relevant and detailed facts and examples
- Connects all arguments to the overall topic in a clear, concise, and organized manner
- Presents the arguments and supporting evidence in a clear, logical manner
- Presents clear, thorough, and accurate information throughout the debate
- Addresses all of the opposing team's arguments with counter-arguments
- Identifies any weakness in the opposing team's arguments
- Constructs strong and relevant counter-arguments using accurate information
- Presents strong and persuasive arguments throughout the debate
- Summarizes the arguments in the closing statement

Introducing the Characters

A novel's characters are what make its story relatable, so the reader must care about them in order to stay motivated to continue reading the book. The author introduces the characters to the reader through a process called characterization. Taking place early in the novel, characterization can be carried out in several ways. Some writers rely on the characters' own words, called dialogue, to show the reader their personalities, while others characterize a story's players through their actions.

Major Characters in *The Book Thief*

Zusak uses a variety of characterization methods in *The Book Thief*, including providing the reader with Liesel's back story. Instead of starting the narrative when she arrives on Himmel Street, Zusak begins Liesel's story on the train. The reader experiences Liesel's brother's death along with her, feeling her overwhelming shock and sadness. Later, when she does arrive at the Hubermann's home, Liesel hears Rosa's surprise that "the boy" isn't with her. Liesel had thought that her mother had sent her away out of grief, but she soon discovers that giving her—and her brother—up had been the plan all along.

As Liesel starts to settle into Molching, Zusak moves on to other methods of characterization for both her and other characters. For instance, the reader learns that Rosa is someone to be reckoned with when the narrator shares that, "Nobody wanted to be the one to tell Rosa Hubermann that the boy didn't survive the trip. In fact, no one ever really wanted to tell her anything."

Dynamic characters such as Liesel change throughout the course of a story, frequently as a result of its conflicts. Rosa is another example of a dynamic character, as she softens through the family's experiences with Liesel and Max. In fact, the ways that Rosa changes actually prompt some of the ways that Liesel changes. She bonds with her foster father quickly, but by the middle of the book, she has learned that Rosa cares for them all deeply as well.

Static characters do not change, but they are essential for driving a story forward. Franz Duetscher, the leader of Rudy's Hitler youth group, is a static character. Franz does not merely follow the motions of showing his allegiance to the Führer, but he also believes in it with his entire being. A cruel young man, he takes pleasure in harassing Rudy at every opportunity.

ACTIVITIES

Weblink

Character Analysis of Rosa Hubermann

Review a character analysis of Rosa and debate her role in *The Book Thief*.

1. Rosa is a complex character. While she can be violent and insulting at times, she also displays care and concern. How do these contradictory traits affect the reader's opinion of her? Give textual evidence to support your claims.
2. Do you Rosa is a cold, harsh character or a loving character? Is it possible for her to fall into both categories? Why or why not?

More

Character Development in *The Book Thief*

Analyze the characters in *The Book Thief* using the descriptions on the character map and excerpts from each character. Then, choose a character and answer the following questions.

1. Which of the writer's techniques are most effective at revealing this character's traits? Why?
2. In what ways is the characterization of this character ineffective? What could be done to improve this character's function in the novel? Defend your ideas with evidence.

Creating a Literary Device Analysis Booklet

Students will analyze the author's use of a literary device in the novel, and create a booklet to present this analysis. An exemplary literary device analysis booklet will meet the following criteria.

- Defines the chosen literary device accurately and in detail
- Places the definition of the literary device at the beginning of the booklet
- Provides strong, specific examples of how this literary device is used in the novel
- Describes examples in detail, with quotations properly integrated
- Includes thorough analysis of the use, purpose, and effectiveness of each example of how the chosen literary device is used in the novel
- Arranges all pages logically
- Examples are organized chronologically
- Provides no more than one example and its analysis per page
- Creates a neat, well-organized, and attractive booklet
- Booklet is colorful and displays the student's creativity
- Uses illustrations to represent the chosen literary device and the examples of how it is used in the novel

The Art of Storytelling

Writers have many tools for telling their stories. These different devices, and the ways that an author chooses to utilize them, are what make each story unique. The same narrative may be thrilling or boring, depending on how the writer decides to tell it, and which literary tools the writer employs.

Structure of a Narrative

Although they must be creative in the ways they utilize literary tools, most writers know that sticking to an arrangement called Freytag's Pyramid is the best way to structure a novel. This template for creating the plot of a story helps keep the narrative on track. This dramatic arrangement consists of five main parts. Zusak followed each of these steps in writing *The Book Thief*.

Freytag's Pyramid

2 Rising Action
The events that create increased drama or tension.

3 Climax
The moment of greatest tension in the story's action, when the protagonist faces his or her conflict.

4 Falling Action
The events that take place after the climax, leading to the end of the story.

1 Exposition
The beginning of the story, where the characters and setting are introduced.

5 Resolution
The end of the story, when the conflicts are resolved and the action comes to a conclusion.

Plot

Plot is a collective term for the events that take place in a story. These events move the story from one point to the next. Together, they make up the plotline. A well-organized plotline makes the narrative flow naturally.

Plot Points in The Kiss (A Childhood Decision Maker)

1. Liesel joins the other kids on Himmel Street for a soccer game.
2. The kids always make the new kid play the position of goalie, including Liesel.
3. Although Rudy is used to making penalty kicks without much effort, he misses when he tries to score on Liesel.
4. Liesel starts walking to school with Rudy and his siblings.
5. Rudy shows Liesel where Jewish families live on the "road of yellow stars" and how their doors are marked with the Star of David.
6. Liesel learns that shopkeeper Frau Diller demands that all customers *heil*, or salute, Hitler before entering her establishment.
7. Liesel and the group of children stop at a tailor shop, which she learns is owned by their father.
8. Rudy challenges Liesel to a race and tells her that he is going to kiss her if he wins, but they end up reaching the finish line at the same moment.

Literary Devices

Literary devices are the tools a writer uses to tell a story. These tools fall into two categories called literary elements and literary techniques. Nearly all stories contain the same elements, which help make the narrative interesting. Each writer may use a different combination of literary techniques, however. These tools are what give writers their individual voices.

Literary Elements

A literary element is a feature of a narrative that appears in almost every work of literature. The narrative needs these major features in order to be effective and engaging.

MORAL
A moral is a lesson that the reader receives from the story.

Action
The action in a narrative is what happens in the story.

Narrative Point of View
The narrative point of view is the **perspective** from which a story is told.

Literary Techniques

Literary techniques are the various ways a writer can manipulate language to convey meaning or to create a distinct style.

Metaphor
A metaphor is a symbol.

Personification
When a writer ascribes human qualities to a non-human character, it is called personification.

Simile
A simile describes one thing by comparing it to another using the word "like" or "as."

ACTIVITIES

Video

Hay festival: Markus Zusak on The Book Thief
Learn more about Zusak and *The Book Thief* by watching this video.

1. In the video, Zusak discusses the narrative point of view of the novel. Why did he choose Death to narrate the story? How effective is Death in this role? Cite examples from the text to back up your position.
2. Zusak explains that since Adolf Hitler destroyed people with words, Liesel's theft of books is a way to steal the words back, and write her own story. How does this relate to the moral of the story?

More

Examples of Literary Techniques from the Novel
Analyze the author's use of literary techniques and how they contribute to the narrative of *The Book Thief*.

1. Choose one literary technique used in the novel. In what particular way did the author use this literary technique? How effective was its usage?
2. What arguments can be made for the use of your chosen literary technique in a text? If this technique were overused or underutilized, what effect might it have on an author's work?

Theme in the Novel

Every novel has at least one theme, or main idea. Many, including *The Book Thief*, have more than one theme. Some are straightforward, while others require the reader to look deeper to identify and fully understand them. A novel's subject is not its theme. Two novels can be about completely different subjects, yet share a common theme. It may take readers most of the book to uncover the theme, as they learn about this main idea along with the characters.

Values

Values are intrinsic to a novel's theme. Part of the purpose of characterization is to show the reader the characters' values. These beliefs are the foundation of each character's behavior, and they typically determine how the characters manage the story's conflict. The things a character says and does reveal much about his or her values. Some characters even experience a changing of their values over the course of the story.

Major Themes of *The Book Thief*

Through Liesel, Zusak shows the reader the power that words can have. In the beginning of the story, nine-year-old Liesel cannot read, and she is made to feel powerless and embarrassed by this shortcoming at school. When Hans teaches her to read, Liesel starts to realize all the things that this ability allows her to learn, and she begins to see that words can manipulate people as well. She sees how Hitler uses words as weapons to frighten people into supporting his cause. She, however, continues to use words for good instead of evil, such as when she calms her neighbors during a bombing raid by reading aloud to them.

The Kindness and Cruelty of People

"As it turned out, Ilsa Hermann not only gave Liesel Meminger a book that day. She also gave her a reason to spend time in the basement—her favorite place, first with Papa, then with Max. She gave her a reason to write her own words, to see that words had also brought her to life."

Ilsa Hermann's Little Black Book

ACTIVITIES

Weblink

How to Write an Analysis of Theme

Evaluate the blog post about identifying and analyzing themes.

1. Why is it helpful to consider theme when analyzing other aspects of literature? Do you think it is true that the importance of theme in literature can be overstated? Give reasons for your answer.
2. It is suggested that themes can be more easily identified by examining how other parts of the story are related, such as tone, values, style, characters, motivation, and plot. How does Zusak bring all of these parts together in *The Book Thief* to make a unified whole?

More

Major and Secondary Themes

Analyze the author's development of themes over the course of the novel.

1. Choose a secondary theme from this spread and analyze its appearances in the novel. How does this theme first emerge? Which is the most poignant example of this theme in the novel?
2. What particular commentary might the author be making about life as a result of this theme's presence in the text? Explain and defend your ideas.
3. Choose a major theme presented on pages 16–17. In what ways does your chosen secondary theme relate to this major theme? Does it deepen or detract from the major theme? How or in what way?

The Nazis Forced People to Hide

"They walked around a few corners onto Himmel Street, and Alex said, 'Son, you can't go around painting yourself black, you hear?'

Rudy was interested, and confused...'Why not, Papa?'

'Because they'll take you away.'

'Why?'

'Because you shouldn't want to be like black people or Jewish people or anyone who is...not *us*.'...

They walked on in silence for a while, until Rudy said, 'I just wish I was like Jesse Owens, Papa.'

This time, Mr. Steiner placed his hand on Rudy's head and explained, 'I know, son...'"

The Jesse Owens Incident

Appreciation of Life

"On Christmas Eve, Liesel brought down a double handful of snow as a present for Max. 'Close your eyes,' she'd said. 'Hold out your hands.' As soon as the snow was transferred, Max shivered and laughed, but he still didn't open his eyes. He only gave the snow a quick taste, allowing it to sink into his lips."

The Snowman

Secondary Themes

Other themes in *The Book Thief* include family, friendships, and love. Liesel learns that family is about more than blood as she begins to care deeply for her foster parents and Max. She also discovers the importance of friendship through her relationships with Rudy and Ilsa Hermann. Rudy feels more than friendship for Liesel, but he is killed in a bombing before he is able to tell her. The closest he comes is asking her for a kiss, which she finally gives his lifeless body after Death has taken her friend. Her love for Rudy and her adopted family members survives the war, however, as she carries it with her for the rest of her long life.

RUBRIC

Creating a Symbolism Poster

Students will choose one of the other symbols listed on page 19 and analyze its role in the novel. They will then create a poster to present their analysis. An exemplary symbolism poster will meet the following criteria.

- Presents a clear purpose that is conveyed throughout the poster
- Shows an understanding of the concept of symbolism and the role it has in the novel
- Provides an in-depth analysis of what the symbol represents
- Discusses the role the symbol has in the novel
- Clearly indicates where the symbol appears in the novel
- Uses specific, detailed examples from the text to support the analysis
- Makes clear connections to the text
- Properly integrates all quotations
- Organizes the information in a logical, easy-to-read manner
- Includes high-quality graphics that relate to the symbol and effectively enhance understanding of the topic
- Features clear and concise writing
- Uses correct spelling, grammar, and punctuation
- Clearly labels items of importance
- Headings and subheadings are clear and easy to read
- Uses layout to creatively enhances the information
- Creates a poster that is attractive in terms of layout, design, and organization
- Shows a strong effort by the student

Symbolism in the Novel

If authors came right out and told the reader everything in a literal way, books would not be nearly as interesting. Part of what many readers enjoy most is considering the various symbols that writers use to emphasize their stories. Symbolism is a literary technique that helps the reader better understand the themes in the story. Some symbols are tangible objects, while others are merely concepts.

The Grave Digger's Handbook

"There was something black and rectangular lodged in the snow. Only the girl saw it. She bent down and picked it up and held it firmly in her fingers. The book had silver writing on it."

Arrival on Himmel Street

Liesel's Books as a Symbol

Among the most important symbols in *The Book Thief* are the books that Liesel steals and her relationship with them. What the books stand for changes greatly over time. At the start of the story, Liesel takes *The Grave Digger's Handbook*, even though she cannot read it. The mere act of taking the book symbolizes the control over her life that she wants so badly. Even though she cannot read the words at the time, she is compelled to take it. Later, the handbook becomes a symbol of her victory when it becomes the first book she reads from beginning to end.

When Liesel steals *The Shoulder Shrug* at the book burning, it becomes symbolic of her unwillingness to go along with the ceremony's ominous sentiment. As she begins to feel uneasy with the Nazis' agenda, she steals the book as a way of rebelling against it, even if the act must be a secret one. The books she later borrows from Ilsa Hermann symbolize Liesel's growing power over her own mind in an era where nearly everything else in her life is dictated by the war.

What Other Symbols Appear in the Novel?

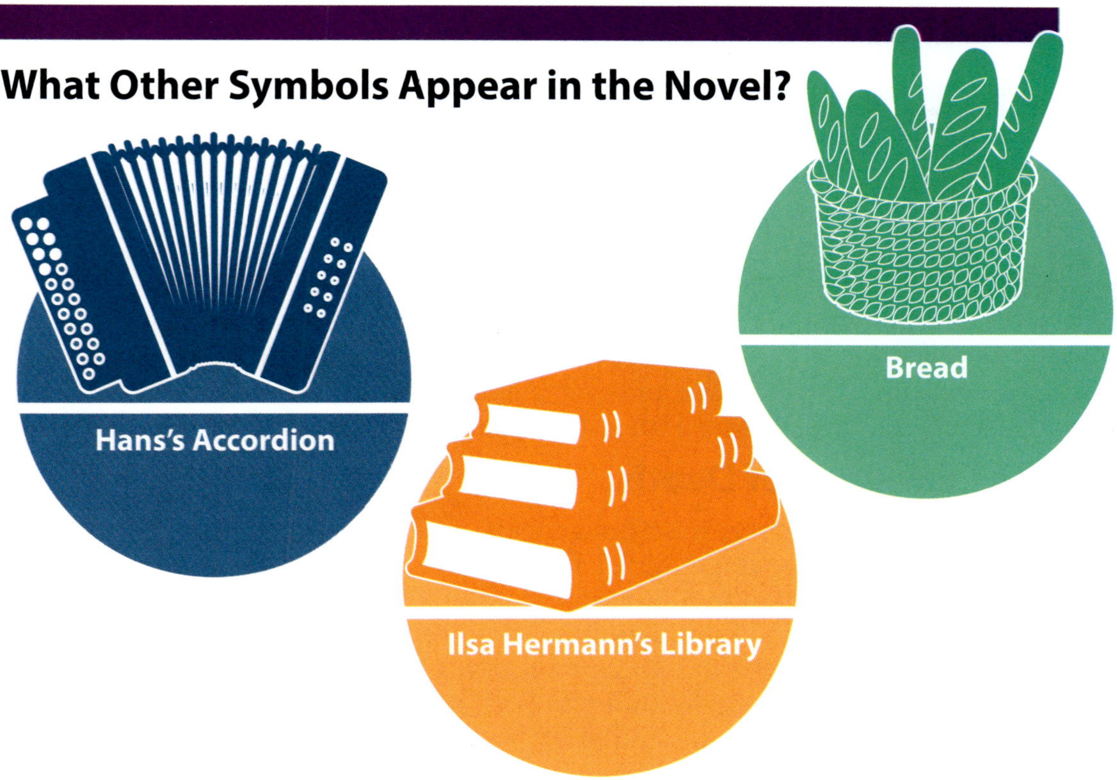

Other Symbols in the Novel

Hans's Accordion

Hans's accordion is a symbol of his kind and uplifting nature, as he plays it for others to lift their mood. In a world filled with so much sadness, it brings happiness to those who hear its music. The instrument is also a symbol of the debt Hans feels to Max's father. The accordion belonged to Erik Vandenburg when he was alive, and it was passed on to Hans after he died. When Hans met Erik during World War I, Hans didn't even know how to play it.

Bread

When characters in *The Book Thief* give bread to the starving Jews, this simple food becomes a symbol of both kindness and of life itself. In another situation, giving food to starving people would seem like a small act, certainly not a selfless one, but in the novel, the act goes against the rigid rules of the Nazis. If people are caught giving bread to a Jew, they will be severely punished, so they risk their own safety to give sustenance to another person.

Ilsa Hermann's Library

When the mayor's wife tells Liesel she can borrow books from her home's library, she gives the young girl access to a vast amount of knowledge. The immense number and variety of books symbolize that knowledge. They also symbolize the power that Liesel feels in knowing she can read and learn as much as she wants.

ACTIVITIES

More

What Symbols Appear in the Novel?
Assess the author's use of symbolism in the novel.

1. Choose an example from the chart and analyze what this symbol represents. For which character is this symbol the most poignant in the novel? For which character is the symbol least poignant? Argue your opinions with clear reasons.
2. How is this symbol used or reflected in the novel's themes? Illustrate the ways in which the author's use of language deepens or weakens the meaning of the symbol. Explain and defend your ideas.

Weblink

The Complete Guide to Symbolism
Examine the blog post discussing the usage of symbolism in literature.

1. Contrast and compare examples of analytical descriptions of feelings and sensory descriptions using symbolism from the novel. Which kind is more effective in the novel? Provide reasons for your ideas.
2. Should analytical descriptions play a considerable role in the language of a novel? Why or why not?

The Use of Language

Language can be used in many ways to tell a story. This arrangement of words does more than just convey the events of a narrative. It also sets the mood of the book for a reader. Careful, detailed descriptions of settings and characters, for example, can paint a vivid world that readers can visualize more and more with each word. In other cases, short, blunt dialogue can show the reader who the characters are, and even a bit about what they are experiencing, in an instant. Zusak used more of the latter type of style when writing *The Book Thief*.

The Language of Death

Making Death the narrator was a bold choice, and Zusak wasted no opportunity to make this storyteller sound as dark and eerie as any reader might imagine Death to be. At the same time, the reader isn't nearly as frightened by Death as by the situation in which Liesel finds herself. Death pulls no punches. On the very first page, he states, "I most definitely *can* be cheerful. I can be amiable. Agreeable. Affable. And that's only the A's. Just don't ask me to be nice. Nice has nothing to do with me." The reader instantly becomes curious about the story that Death wishes to tell.

Zusak's language is a profound part of what makes *The Book Thief* such a unique novel. Just when readers immerse themselves into the character's world, the author pulls them back out to remind them who is telling the story. Toward the end of the novel, Death admits, "It's probably fair to say that in all the years of Hitler's reign, no person was able to serve the *Führer* as loyally as me."

Action-Based Descriptions

As Zusak moves forward with the telling of this story, he paints his picture with descriptions of the characters. In most cases, though, it is the actions of the characters that tell the reader the most. When Zusak describes how Liesel gets to know Hans, he does not spend much time telling the reader what Hans looks like. Instead, he writes, "Every morning just after two o'clock, she fell asleep again to the smell of him. It was a mixture of dead cigarettes, decades of paint, and human skin." This certainly is not a pretty description, but it shows the reader what a dedicated father figure Hans is—right there by the young girl's side just in case she has another nightmare. Better yet, the reader can almost smell that odd mixture of scents that make up the character, just as Liesel can.

Conversational Tone

The author makes Death seem real to the reader by giving him a personality. While the overall tone of the book is a sad one, Death uses sarcasm, wit, and even a bit of humor as he tells his tale. He speaks to the reader using a conversational tone, in the way a person might tell a story to a friend. He is comfortable, skipping around from one time period to another, and even apologizing for revealing too much too soon at certain points. The author's choice of informal language makes Death seem almost human himself.

Zusak uses bold, succinct language for his narrator, which helps the reader see Death as an impartial storyteller. Since Death's language is never flowery or elaborate, the reader can trust him more. He does not try too hard to convince the reader of anything. He simply tells, then shows through action and dialogue. There is a noticeable shift in the tone when the narrator speaks directly to the reader, which allows the audience to get caught up in the story at times, perhaps even forgetting who is telling it.

An Aside to the Reader

"By the way—I like this human idea of the grim reaper. I like the **scythe**. It amuses me."

The Heavyweight Champion of the School-Yard

Rudy

An Announcement to the Audience

"A SMALL ANNOUNCEMENT ABOUT RUDY STEINER. He didn't deserve to die the way he did."

The Floating Book (Part I)

ACTIVITIES

Document

Death & All His Friends: Narration in Markus Zusak's *The Book Thief*

Review the thesis by Caitlin Mattera, exploring Zusak's novel.

1. Who do you think is the intended audience for this document? Why? Are the tone and language used appropriate for this audience? Explain your answer.
2. What are the main points of the document and how are they presented? Are these points conveyed effectively to the reader? Why or why not?

First Hand

Call Me Death: Odd Narrator of a Girl's Story

Learn more about Death as the narrator of *The Book Thief* in this National Public Radio interview from April 2, 2016.

1. The interviewer claims that Death's introduction at the beginning of the story is some of the most evocative writing in the book. Do you agree with this assessment? Give reasons to support your opinion.
2. How would the story have been affected if Zusak had made a more traditional choice of narrator? What would the novel be like if Liesel told her own story instead of Death?

RUBRIC

Writing a Review

Students will write a review of the novel. An exemplary review will meet the following criteria.

- Grabs the reader's attention with a creative headline
- Begins with an engaging lead to pull the reader into the article
- Introduces the title of the novel, the author, and the genre
- Provides a brief plot description that does not give away the entire story, and makes the reader want to learn more about the novel
- Supports arguments about the novel with accurate and detailed information
- Organizes the review and its arguments in a concise, clear, and logical manner
- Fits the format and style of a review
- Follows the conventions of print or online journalism
- Demonstrates creativity in their approach
- Writes with a unique, engaging voice and perspective
- Provides fresh insight into the novel
- Provides an honest, authentic opinion on the novel
- Gives a clear recommendation on the novel, backed up by specific textual evidence
- Uses correct spelling, grammar, and punctuation

Impact of the Novel at the Time of Publishing

The Book Thief made a huge impression on readers of all ages when it was published, although some people thought the tale was a bit dark to be a children's book. However, others thought that having Death as its narrator made the book even more appealing. As noted in *Popular Appeal: Books and Films in Contemporary Youth Culture*, "Death is an appealing narrator because he is so different to the usual expectations."

An Instant Award Winner

The National Jewish Book Council named *The Book Thief* its recipient for the 2006 Children's and Young Adults' Literature Award. This was just one of several awards Zusak received for the novel, soon after its publication. Critics from influential newspapers such as *The New York Times* and the *Washington Post* also praised the book.

The Meaning of the Cover

To some people, the dominoes about to be toppled on the book's cover seemed an odd choice for a book about Nazi Germany—until they read the book. The graphic relates to a point in the story in which the Nazis approach Rudy's parents about the idea of him attending their school. While the adults talk, Rudy and his sisters play a game of dominoes, and this innocent game becomes a symbol for the many people who "fall" during the course of the book, including Rudy himself.

Zusak's Low Expectations

Zusak worried that people would be put off by the book's subject and its length. In an interview with *Ezra Magazine*, he explained, "I thought it would be my least successful book, mainly because I imagined that if someone actually liked it and tried to recommend it to their friends, they'd be asked, 'Well, what's it about?' That person then has to say, 'Well it's set in Nazi Germany, it's narrated by Death, nearly everyone dies...and it's 560 pages long—you'll love it.'"

Criticized for its Violence

It would be difficult to tell a story about Nazi Germany without acknowledging the violence that took place during World War II. Still, some parents thought that Zusak's depictions of these historical events were too harsh for young readers, and demanded that the book be issued a rating for its violence to keep it out of the hands of kids under a certain age. Other adults saw this act as censorship, and argued that the novel's historical accuracy outweighed concerns about Zusak's treatment of topics such as the Nazis' cruelty. Despite its criticisms, the novel has never appeared on the challenged books list.

The Book Thief was made into **a film eight years after the book's publication**.

Zusak is quoted as saying, **"I was a total mess when I was writing those last 50 pages** [of *The Book Thief*]."

The novel spent more than **500 weeks** on the ***New York Times* Best Seller List**.

ACTIVITIES

Document

Fighting for Their Lives

Analyze the review from *The New York Times* by John Green, published on May 14, 2006, exploring his views on *The Book Thief*.

1. What is the tone of the review? Green describes *The Book Thief* as potentially "life-changing, because...[it] offers us a believable, hard-won hope." Do you agree that the hope embodied in Liesel is "unassailable," as Green claims? Give examples from the novel to support your answer.
2. According to Green, the character of Death "is so innocuous that he's not very absorbing." Is this a fair assessment? Why or why not?

First Hand

Interview with Markus Zusak, Author of The Book Thief and I Am the Messenger

Examine this 2010 interview with Markus Zusak by Cindy Hudson.

1. Hudson points out that while *The Book Thief* is marketed as a young adult book in the United States, it was originally released for adult readers in Zusak's native Australia. What audience do you think is most appropriate and why? Does the novel have qualities that lean more to one demographic or the other, or can it appeal to both? Explain your answer.
2. Zusak was surprised by the success of the novel, stating that he thought it would be his least-read book. Why do you think it has been so well-received?

Impact of the Novel Now

The Book Thief has become one of the most revered books in young adult literature. Like many popular children's books, it has also become a favorite novel of many adults. Years after its release, *The Book Thief* is still a popular choice in classrooms and book clubs in many parts of the world.

New Insights

In an interview for the *Huffington Post* about *The Book Thief*'s 10th anniversary, Zusak discussed his generous use of symbols in the novel. One of the symbols that stands out to him most is his description of Max Vandenburg as being like a bird. Zusak stated, "I used the irony of that idea because he was German but he was imprisoned in his own country; he was a caged bird who needed to hide in order to survive."

The Book Thief has been **translated** into more than **30 languages** across the world.

The Book Thief has sold **more than 10 million** copies worldwide **since its original publication**.

The **$19 million** motion picture adaptation of the book **earned** more than **$76 million** at the box office.

The Motion Picture

Zusak signed a contract for the film rights shortly after the novel's release. At that time, he was not counting on it actually happening, since many books that get signed for this step do not actually make it to the production stage. When the project was finally underway, Zusak said that he was thrilled with the director and cast. He was especially pleased that Geoffrey Rush and Emily Watson would play Hans and Rosa, and he was very impressed with the young actress the producers chose for the role of Liesel—Sophie Nélisse.

A Major Award Winner

The Book Thief's 2013 film adaptation proved to be a huge success. The film was nominated for both an Academy Award and a Golden Globe for its musical score. Sophie Nélisse won the Hollywood Film Festival Spotlight Award, the Satellite Newcomer Award, and the Phoenix Film Critics Society Award for Best Performance by a Youth in a Lead or Supporting Role—Female.

The Losses Were Not Easy

People still come up to Zusak to discuss *The Book Thief*. The characters and events are as real to them as they were to the author when he created them. In an interview with *Paste Magazine*, Zusak shared that readers often ask him about why he killed off certain characters. He justifies this by claiming, "You have to do what's right for the book, not what's right for one character in the book. I also say to them that maybe we wouldn't love those characters as much if they'd survived."

ACTIVITIES

First Hand

MARKUS ZUSAK

10 years of 'The Book Thief'

Examine this interview with Zusak from March 8, 2016, marking the 10th anniversary of *The Book Thief*.

1. In the interview, Zusak says, "These days I've realized that *The Book Thief* is about the stories we read and write, but especially the stories we make." What do you think he means by this observation? How is this exemplified in the novel?
2. Zusak reflects on the characters he created, claiming that although he loved them, he does not miss them. Do you think this is position is unique to creators, or do readers feel similarly when finishing a book? Explain your answer by recounting your experience.

Document

The Book Thief: Film Review

Analyze the review from The Hollywood Reporter by Stephen Farber, published on November 6, 2013, exploring his views on the film adaptation of Zusak's novel.

1. Farber notes that the film is not very dramatic or surprising, which he attributes to Zusak's source material, despite his admission that the screenplay is "overly expository." Do Farber's criticisms apply to the novel, or are these issues due simply to the screenwriter? Give evidence to support your opinion.
2. Farber says that "nothing would work without the performance of the actress cast as Liesel." Why do you think this is the case? What qualities must the actors portraying the other characters display?

RUBRIC

Creating a Timeline

Students will explore a topic related to the novel and create a timeline to present their research on historical events connected to this topic. An exemplary timeline will meet the following criteria.

- Includes the most significant events pertaining to the topic to be compared and analyzed
- Includes interesting events
- Uses accurate information for all events, including date, location, and major details
- Orders the events in a chronological sequence
- Describes each event with accurate, vivid, and specific details
- Presents the topic from three or more perspectives
- Inspires the reader to ask thoughtful questions regarding the events and perspectives presented in the timeline
- Uses correct spelling, grammar, and punctuation
- Presents the timeline in a visually attractive and striking manner
- Presents the timeline in a neat, organized manner that is logical and easy to follow
- Uses creativity to present the timeline in an engaging manner
- Effectively communicates the historical information relating to the topic
- Supports each event with reliable sources
- Expresses a clear purpose for creating the timeline
- Enhances the reader's understanding of the topic
- Includes a correctly formatted bibliography of all sources used to create the timeline

Perspectives on World War II Germany

One of the strongest themes in *The Book Thief* is the survival of love and friendship through the worst of times. Zusak shows that family and friends do not put their lives on hold for the Führer or his war. Rather, they live as best they can in the circumstances forced upon them, and they find moments of great joy amidst their equally profound, and often abundant, sorrow.

Timeline of Jewish Oppression in Germany

1919 The Treaty of Versailles is signed.

1935 Through the Nuremberg Race Laws, Hitler passes anti-Semitic legislation that immediately **segregates** Jews from other Germans.

1910s **1920s** **1930s**

1933 Hitler is appointed Chancellor of Germany.

1934 Hitler abolishes the office of president of Germany, becoming the nation's absolute dictator.

1936 The Summer Olympics take place in Berlin. American Jewish runners Marty Glickman and Sam Stoller are replaced by Jesse Owens and Ralph Metcalfe the day before the 4x100-meter relay.

Writing a young adult book set in Nazi Germany is no easy task. Inevitably, people would criticize the author either for being too graphic or for glossing over important details. While the story of *The Book Thief* is fictitious, the backdrop for the novel is all too real. To pretend that Nazi Germany was anything less than horrific would dishonor those who were forced to live through it, and those who did not survive it. This is why many readers believe that the inclusion of mature content is justified, and perhaps even necessary. Novels such as *The Book Thief* help readers to remember and honor the victims of this tragic historic event, which is one of the best ways to make sure that nothing like it ever happens again.

1938 A German decree orders all Jewish-owned businesses to shut down, effectively excluding Jews from the German economy.

1940 The Auschwitz Concentration Camp is established.

1940s

1939 Germany invades Poland, triggering the beginning of World War II.

1945 World War II officially ends when first Germany, and later Japan, surrender.

"All the News That's Fit to Print."
The New York Times.
EXTRA
GERMAN ARMY ATTACKS POLAND; CITIES BOMBED, PORT BLOCKADED; DANZIG IS ACCEPTED INTO REICH

1941 All Jews over the age of six years are forced to wear a badge that identifies them as Jewish.

ACTIVITIES

Transparency–Timeline

Timeline of Jewish Oppression in Germany

Examine the historical and cultural contexts shown on the timeline. Then, contrast and correlate its elements with the themes and events presented in *The Book Thief.*

1. In what ways can historical events, culture, and social mores influence a population's perspective on freedom and oppression? How might these elements have shaped the way a reader in the mid-2000s interpreted the novel?
2. How might the era in which Markus Zusak wrote *The Book Thief* have influenced the novel's themes and settings? Where in the novel is this most evident? Explain your reasoning.
3. Which current events, changes in laws, new ideas, or political discussions are shaping people's opinions of freedom and oppression in the United States today? Which ideas and attitudes are still prevailing? Why?
4. How might current events and present perspectives affect the way a reader interprets the novel? Why is it important for readers to understand the era and context in which a novel is written?

RUBRIC

Writing a Comparative Essay

Students will compare two literary devices used in the novel, and then write a comparative essay based on their analysis. An exemplary comparative essay will meet the following criteria.

- Consists of a one-paragraph introduction, three body paragraphs, and a one-paragraph conclusion
- Introduction includes an engaging lead statement about the topic of the essay, more detailed information about the novel, and a one-sentence thesis that specifically states the essay's argument
- Body paragraphs include a topic sentence that refers to the thesis and how the idea appears in the novel, a supporting sentence that points to this part of the novel, textual evidence of this idea from the novel, and analysis of this evidence
- Body paragraphs end with a transition to the next paragraph
- Conclusion refers to the topic of the essay and the three points presented in the body paragraphs, and restates the thesis
- Provides a thorough analysis of the literary devices in question
- Cites strong and thorough textual evidence to support analysis of what the novel says explicitly
- Presents a clear, specific thesis that indicates a high level of critical engagement
- Organizes ideas in a logical manner
- Communicates arguments in a clear, effective manner
- Properly integrates all quotations
- Correctly cites all sources used
- Correctly formats bibliography

Writing a Comparative Essay

The Book Thief includes some fascinating characters and themes. After reading the novel, write a comparative essay to contrast how two literary devices are used in the narrative. You may compare two characters, themes, symbols, or settings. Bear in mind that a comparative essay needs a well-formed argument. You must clearly state both the differences and similarities between the two literary devices you choose to explore. Offer evidence for your position using logical thoughts and quotes from the novel as examples.

How to Analyze and Compare Characters

Use the chart below to guide your comparison between two characters in *The Book Thief*.

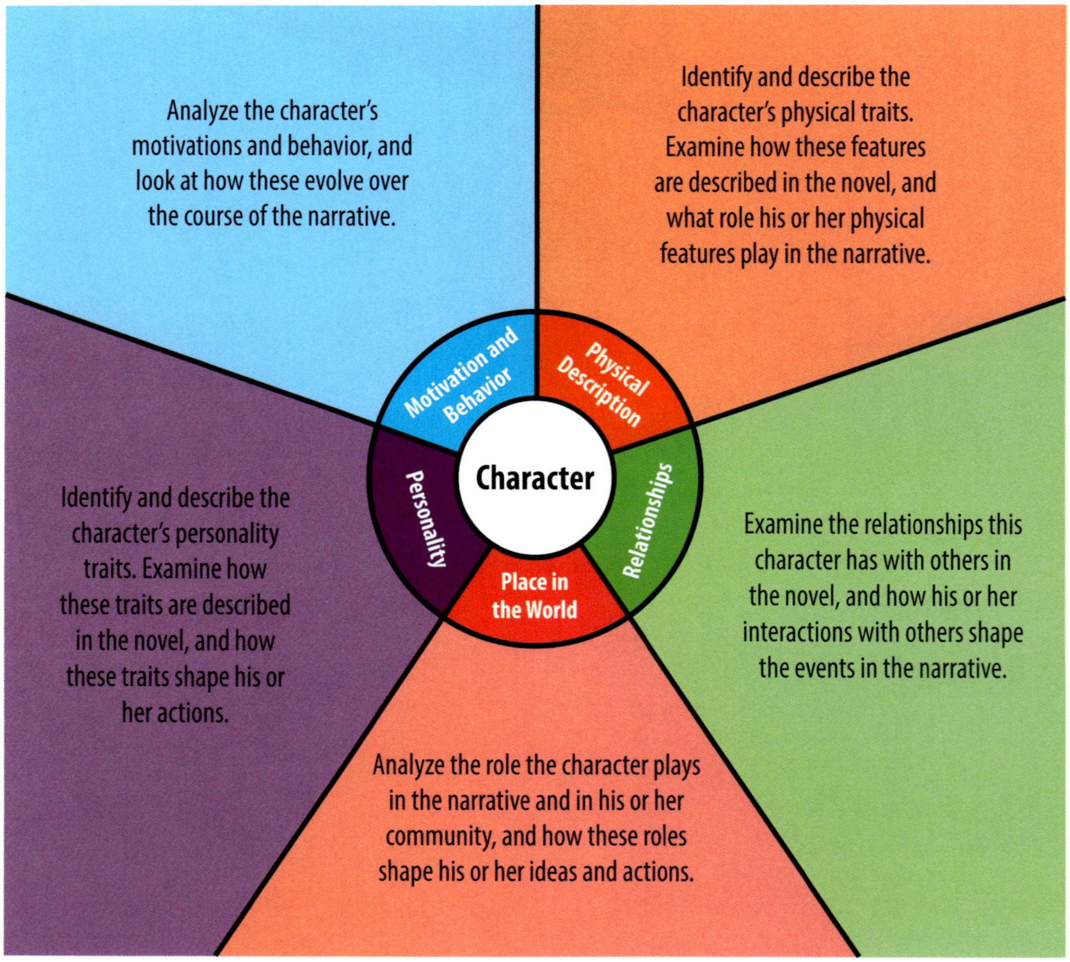

ACTIVITIES

Comparing Liesel Meminger and Max Vandenburg

Liesel Meminger

Personality
- Angry and distrusting at the start of the novel because of all she has lost
- Becomes loving and devoted to her family and friends as the story progresses
- Not afraid to endanger herself to help others in need

Motivation and Behavior
- Trying to gain some control over her life, she becomes a book thief
- Passionate about the people she cares about

Place in the World
- Protagonist
- Learns much about the world through living with her new foster family and hiding a Jew from the Nazis

Relationships
- Daughter to a mother who gave her up
- Sister to Werner, who dies at the beginning of the story
- Foster daughter to Hans and Rosa Hubermann
- Friend to Max and Rudy

Physical Description
- Nine years old as the story begins
- About 15 years old when the story ends, although the reader is told she lives to be an old woman

Max Vandenburg

Place in the World
- Physically weak, but mentally strong
- Overcomes illness to survive the war

Motivation and Behavior
- His anger toward Hitler helps him survive
- His affection for the Hubermanns and Liesel also gives him strength while he is in hiding

Physical Description
- 24 years old at the beginning of the story
- Resembles a bird

Relationships
- Son of Hans's late friend, Erik Vandenburg
- Taken in by Hans and Rosa Hubermann
- Becomes especially close to Liesel

Personality
- Cautious and withdrawn
- Angry about what is happening to him and other Jewish people at Hitler's hands

More

Questions for Character Analysis

Analyze how specific character features, such as conflicts, motivations, relationships, place in the world, and personality affect the plot of *The Book Thief*. Cite strong and thorough textual evidence to support your analysis of what the novel says explicitly as well as the inferences you may have drawn from the novel's setting, themes, and symbols.

Quiz Answers

1. B
2. D
3. B
4. C
5. A
6. C
7. B
8. B
9. C
10. D

Key Words

anti-Semitic: prejudiced against Jews

censorship: the act of controlling reading material and other vehicles for free speech

concentration camps: places where prisoners were held and often tortured before being killed

discrimination: unfair treatment of a person or group, particularly on the basis of prejudice

perspective: certain point of view or position regarding a subject

scythe: a long pole with a curved blade at the end

segregates: separates or divides people

society: an organized community of people interacting with each other

swastikas: emblems of the German Nazi party

Treaty of Versailles: a document signed by the Allied Powers and Germany that officially ended World War I

Literary Terms

action: everything that occurs in a narrative

antagonist: the character who stands in opposition to the protagonist; in some cases, the antagonist creates or represents the conflict that the protagonist faces

characterization: the act of describing a character through the person's appearance and personality

character traits: aspects that make up a character's personality

climax: the moment of greatest tension in the story's action

conflict: a struggle between two or more opposing forces, creating a tension that must be resolved

dialogue: the words spoken between characters in a story

dynamic character: a character who changes throughout a story

exposition: the beginning of the story, where the characters and setting are introduced

falling action: the events that take place after the climax, leading up to the end of the story

Freytag's Pyramid: a narrative structure consisting of five elements; this includes exposition, rising action, climax, falling action, and resolution

literary elements: components of every literary work

literary techniques: unique structures of a literary work

metaphor: a symbol used in a story as a literary technique

mood: the feelings evoked by a story

narrative: a logically arranged series of events presented for an audience; a story

narrator: the character or person telling the story, providing background information and opinions on the events, and connecting the gaps between major events and dialogue

plot: the events that take place in a story

protagonist: the person or thing that acts in opposition to the antagonist

resolution: the end of the story, when the problems are resolved and the action comes to a conclusion

rising action: the events that create increased drama or tension

simile: a comparison between two things

static character: a character who does not display major personality changes

symbolism: a stylistic device using symbols to represent and intensify concepts and ideas

theme: the underlying topic of main idea of a story

Index

LIGHTBOX

SUPPLEMENTARY RESOURCES

Click on the plus icon ⊕ found in the bottom left corner of each spread to open additional teacher resources.

- Download and print the book's quizzes and activities
- Access curriculum correlations
- Explore additional web applications that enhance the Lightbox experience

LIGHTBOX DIGITAL TITLES

Packed full of integrated media

VIDEOS

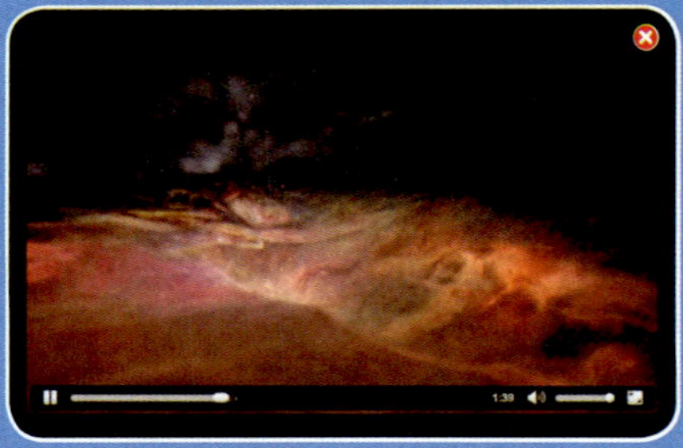

INTERACTIVE MAPS

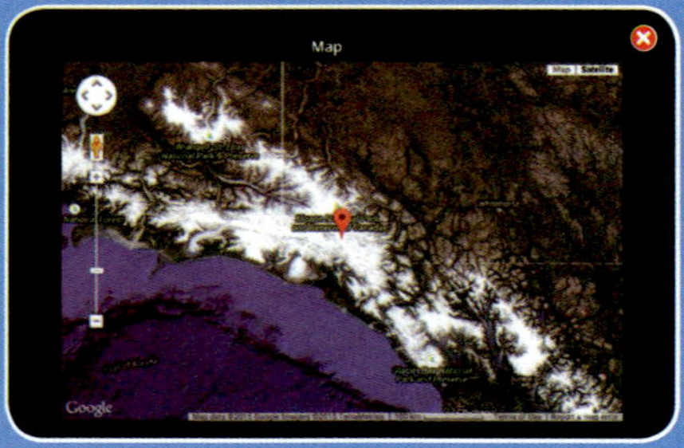

WEBLINKS

SLIDESHOWS

QUIZZES

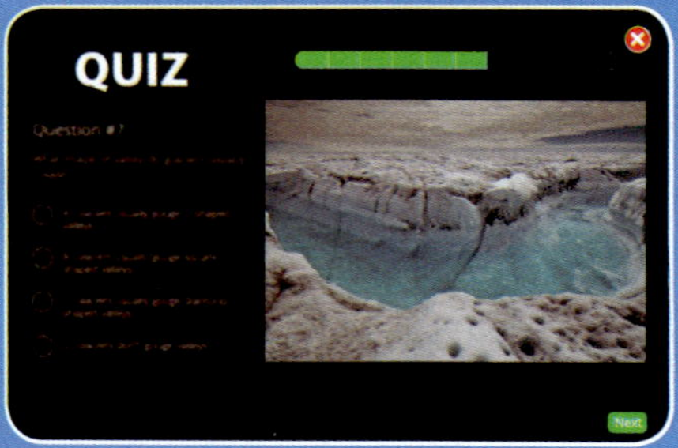

OPTIMIZED FOR

- ✓ TABLETS
- ✓ WHITEBOARDS
- ✓ COMPUTERS
- ✓ AND MUCH MORE!

Published by Smartbook Media Inc.
350 5th Avenue, 59th Floor New York, NY 10118
Website: www.openlightbox.com

Copyright © 2019 Smartbook Media Inc.
All rights reserved. No part of this publication may be reproduced, stored in a retrieval system, or transmitted in any form or by any means, electronic, mechanical, photocopying, recording, or otherwise, without the prior written permission of the publisher.

Library of Congress Cataloging-in-Publication Data
Names: Gagne, Tammy. author. | Gillespie, Katie, author.
Title: The book thief / Tammy Gagne and Katie Gillespie.
Description: New York, NY : Smartbook Media Inc., 2018. | Series: Lightboxliterature studies | Includes index.
Identifiers: LCCN 2017054094 (print) | LCCN 2018004609 (ebook) | ISBN 9781510537095 (Multi-User eBook) | ISBN 9781510537088 (hard cover : alk.paper)
Subjects: LCSH: Zusak, Markus. Book thief--History and criticism. | Zusak, Markus. Book thief--Examinations--Study guides. | Germany--History--1933-1945. | Books and reading in literature. | Storytelling in literature. | Death in literature. | Jews in literature. | World War, 1939-1945--Literature and the war.Classification: LCC PR9619.4.Z87 (ebook) | LCC PR9619.4.Z87 B66 2018 (print) | DDC 823/.92--dc23
LC record available at https://lccn.loc.gov/2017054094

Printed in Brainerd, Minnesota, United States
1 2 3 4 5 6 7 8 9 0 22 21 20 19 18

062018
121017

Editor: Katie Gillespie
Art Director: Terry Paulhus

Every reasonable effort has been made to trace ownership and to obtain permission to reprint copyright material. The publisher would pleased to have any errors or omissions brought to its attention so th they may be corrected in subsequent printings.

The publisher acknowledges Getty Images, iStock, Alamy, and Wikipe Commons as its primary image suppliers for this title.